# A Tear
# From The Corner
# Of Her Eye

Annette Eloise
## Riley Joseph

M.O.R.E. Publishers

St. Louis, Missouri

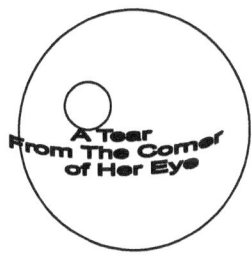

## RAIN

When it rains I feel sadness.

I want to go outside and walk around,

But there is nowhere to go.

I have no money in my pocket.  The rain
is my tear because I feel so alone.

M.O.R.E. Publishers Corp.

www.M.O.R.E.Publishers.com

www.MOREPublishers.biz

Published in the United States

# Where To Find It?

# A Tear From The Corner of Her Eye

**Annette Eloise Riley Joseph**

**"This book is dedicated to my family."**

Also *Dedicated in Memory of*

*Savannah Hicks*

*-*

*Julian W. Riley*

This book is being done in

honor of my Alma Mater

Curtis School

2824 Madison

St. Louis, Missouri

Curtis School
2824 Madison Avenue
St. Louis, MO

Photo by Permission from the St. Louis Public
Schools Archives Department, 1615 Hampton,
St. Louis, Missouri

# Poetry and Prose

©2005

**Annette Eloise Riley Joseph**

# PLATES

You have many plates:

birthday plate, wedding plate, and
anniversary plate.

But you never see a divorce plate,

maybe because it would be broken up in
little pieces.

Plates can be glued back together, but
hearts can't.

# A SMILE

I walk across the water;

Feeling no sorrow; thinking to myself;

Wondering what tomorrow will bring.

Sadness is in the world.

No one happens to know the answer.

Where did the smile go on the people's
faces?

There's no hope.  All the goodness has
dried up.

What can we do to make these faces
smile again?

The only thing we can do is to smile.

# A PRAYER

I walk across the water

feeling no sorrow; thinking to myself,

"I wonder what tomorrow will bring?"

Sadness is in the world.

No one happens to know the answer.

Where did the smile go on the people's
faces?

There's no hope.  All the goodness has
dried up.

What can we do to make these faces
smile again?

The only thing we can do is to have
faith.

# THE OUTER VIEW

-a short story-

There was a boy named James who felt that he was an ugly little boy. He had pointed ears, big, brown eyes, and straight hair. But he had the prettiest smile and a warm heart. He would never look in a mirror, and he felt sad inside. His mother told him that she loved him.

She said, "You are beautiful to me and you have a heart of gold. One day you will find out what I mean."

As time went on, James was getting bigger and bigger, but he never looked in the mirror. One day, a group of people came to his school from a community organization and asked him to join them. He agreed. He left his mother and went to a foreign country where he studied hard and became a doctor.

One of the younger children there needed a leg.  He came back to the States to find the boy an artificial leg. He searched and he searched. Eventually he found one for the little boy.

He went back to the other country and fixed the little boy's leg.  This gesture brought tears to the little boy's eyes. The little boy grew up and helped the doctor with children who were also like him.

James never went back home. But on the holidays, he and the boy would go visit the little boy's mother.

As James got older, there was something he wanted to do that he had never done in his life – look in the mirror at himself.  By that time, he had a beard and long hair. He couldn't see his own face.  Then he cut his hair and beard, and looked in the mirror.  It was as if he looked at his mother. He smiled.

Then the little boy who now is a man said to James, "You have a heart of gold because if it weren't for you, I wouldn't be walking today and helping people as myself.  If God didn't make people like you, this would be a sad world."

## Moral of the Story

*To hide from oneself is very difficult.  James could have found out much earlier in his life that if he only looked in the mirror, he would have seen the beautiful person that everyone saw, including the little crippled boy that became a full-bodied man, thanks to James.*

# A MONSTER

We are good stock. Why do we complain so much about nothing?

I think we just like hearing our voices in our minds. We have taken life for granted and have become greedy about the air and the land.

We stopped caring about what's important to us.

We have taken money for affection.

We have taken cruelness for hatred.

We have taken madness and we use it as being sane.

We turned happiness into sadness.

We are no longer human beings.

We each have become what we we're
afraid of — a monster.

# FINDING YOURSELF

This story is about a girl I use to know.  We grew up in the same neighborhood.  We went to the same school.  Our parents knew each other.  But this girl was going through a different problem growing up, than I did.  She had a handicap.

She walked like a duck.  The children made fun of her everyday when she went to school.  None of the boys wanted to be seen with her because of her handicap.  She wanted a boyfriend just as everybody else.

She even had surgery done on her feet, but things didn't change.  She was still teased.  She started being in her own world, becoming the school clown, and not caring about her grades or life itself.  Then she prayed that someone would care about her.  She used to go off by herself to the park with no shoes on her feet – walking through the grass, asking God to let her find someone to love her.  As she got older, she started getting a pretty figure, but her handicap kept haunting her because people would come up to her and ask, "Why do you walk so funny?"

She was called Cripple Tom, brick feet and duck walk.  She started feeling more self-pity until one day she saw a drunken man with crutches, but with no legs.  He was using his crutches to get around and still taking a drink.

She wiped the tears from her eyes and said, "I will never feel sorry for myself again."

Her parents moved out of the neighborhood.  She went to high school and it was different because no one knew about her handicap.

Then her life took many journeys. Every job she did, involved helping other people.  Some people were as she –

inflicted.  However, she felt she was giving a little back, but that was her secret.

Everyone doesn't have to know what you have been through to help others.  Helping is what makes you feel good.  There are good people in this world.  Sometimes they can be just around the corner.

So whatever you think, there is always someone hurting from teasing. Think about people whose life might be worse than yours.  Look up in the sky and pray for them because there's someone praying for you.  Remember that prayers do get answered.

If you're wondering what happened to my friend, understand that she got married and had four children.

She was blessed because none of her children had her birth defect. She married someone just like her.

# CHAIN

Chains come to connect each other.

Chains make a family.

The chains get bigger and bigger.

When the chains break, the circle must
get fixed.

Just as when someone dies,

A new member of the family comes in

and the circle is formed again.

# A STAR WITHIN YOURSELF

You Black child, when you were born,

You had a star in your eye.

You Black child, you are taught to be tough.

You Black child, you live in a house

that your parents can afford, but people tell
you, you live in a dump.

You Black child, you are told

"Don't expect nothing."

You Black child, don't let your fire burn out.

Don't let anyone tell you that dreams don't
come true.

You Black child, you don't need heroes.

You Black child, you are a hero.

You Black child, pick yourself up, wash your face and say to yourself that "I'm a hero because I'm going to make the dreams come true.

I may not have the best, but I'm reaching for the best.

When it all comes to the end of the road,

I'll be facing me."

## ALL ABOUT SELF

Are you about material things?

Are you just trying to show off?

Just because you may look good,

Doesn't mean that you are good.

Everything that shines, doesn't mean it's gold.

In other words,

You are ugly on the inside

because you can't deal with everyday life.

The clothes don't make the person.

The person makes the clothes.

When you think about it, are you happy?

Having material things is what you got.

That's why you are all alone.  You have the clothes.

So I guess that's all that matters.

at a lounge, and they were having a talent show.  So I got on stage, started singing, and started telling little stories.  I felt a draft.  I thought a door was opened.  The people started laughing and laughing.  I knew my joke wasn't that funny.

I looked down.  My pants were at my feet.  The elastic had broken on my pants.  I was frozen.  How could I get out of this situation?  What could I do?"

I picked up my pants and ran.  I didn't stop until I got home.  I was hoping that no one knew me at the lounge.  I was embarrassed.  I went to my job the next day and what did I see on my desk?  There was a picture of me with my pants at my feet!

Someone had left a note on my desk saying, "You gave a good show. Hope to see your show again."

If they only knew - that was my first and my last show.  So, if you're looking for me, I'll be at the lake with two birds swimming around each other.  I will never complain about being bored. When you get bored, you get into trouble.

# AN INDIAN CRY

First, you stole my land.

Then you killed my people.

I thought I would have peace,

But there's no peace on my land.

Then you broke my spirit.

Then you beat me down.

You broke the light that stood in my
heart.

Now I'm just a legend in history books.

# A STRANGE EXPERIENCE

One day, I was sitting at my yard table. A bird came to my table and took my toast out of my hand. I was very surprised that the bird did this. I shook my head and said to myself, "I can't believe what just happened."

The next day, I sat at my table and a squirrel grabbed my soda. The squirrel ran up the tree as if he was laughing at me. I wasn't going up that tree to get my soda, and then fall down on my fat butt.

Then there was a knock at my door. A lady was asking me to give a little change for a charity. I gave the change to the lady and children. I thought I had more change, so I could buy me another soda. I had given all of my change to the lady and the children. So, I couldn't get me a soda. That day wasn't my day.

So I had a plan, I got some toast and threw it in the yard and I watched the bird run to the toast and the squirrel ran for the bread. Then cats started coming in my yard and started chasing the bird and squirrel from the bread. I couldn't believe what I was seeing in my yard. Then the next day, I went to my table. A small, little boy was sitting at my table. He said, "Look at all these animals in the yard. Is there something special about your yard?"

I had different people and animals coming to my house. I told him I liked feeding the birds and that I didn't know squirrels liked soda. I knew that all of us were God's creatures. The little boy looked at me and said, "Can I come back tomorrow?"

"Yes," I said.

The next day, the little boy brought a cake, soda, and his toys. He went and sat in the grass with cake, and soda and toys. He asked me for a bowl. He poured the soda in a small bowl and sliced the cake into small pieces. He laid his toys out in the grass. He set everything up as if the grass was a tablecloth.

The first creatures that showed up were the birds. Then the squirrel came, and then the cat. I was scared for the child, but he wasn't scared. The bird was eating the cake and so was the cat. The squirrel was drinking the soda and the little boy was playing with his toy.  If I had a camera, I would have taken their picture.  The strange thing about this was no one was fighting or arguing.  Each little living thing was content with what he had.  That just showed me that adults don't know everything.

## STAY PUT

I was looking at two birds at the lake and they kept swimming around each other. Then they came where I was standing. They looked me up and down, and then they went back to the middle of the lake.

Then other people started coming to the lake setting up to catch some fishes. It started out with two birds and me, then the place was crowded just that fast. No wonder the birds stared at me because they knew it wasn't going to be quiet too much longer. There would be music playing, kids running, and people drinking and eating. You couldn't even find a quiet place anymore.

So I started walking and looking at people, passing them by, wondering what to do with myself, bored to death wondering what I could do. I stopped

# A CHANGED MIND

One day, I wanted to leave my
hometown.

I took a walk around the whole city in
one day.

People spoke, but my mind was
somewhere else.

I felt out of place. There was something
missing.
I felt a sense of loss.

All of a sudden, I saw this star.

# FIGURE ME OUT

I'm a flower.

I don't feel as if I should be in this place.

I don't look like a flower.

I'm not yellow as a sunflower.
I'm not purple like a tulip.

I'm not red like a rose.

So what am I?

Why am I here between these flowers?

I have no color.

I have no shape.

What am I?

I'm a weed.

# CHANGING THOUGHTS

I remember

a time when a person

could offer you a piece of bread.

Now they offer you the door.

I remember

a time you could spend with the fellows.

Now they don't even want you around.

I remember

a time you got invited to family

reunions.

Now you don't even hear from them,

just because you are out of a job –

no fault of your own.

Next,

you are looked down on

because you have no money to spend.

You stand-alone
with your changing thoughts –
Thoughts
you never thought you would have.

# GROWING UP

Life has many sorrows.

Why do so many people think it is a
crime to be happy?

Why are so many people unfeeling
toward each other?

People don't want to be affectionate
because so many of us have been hurt
as a little child.

That little child is still scared of opening
up its heart.

Why are we so afraid of life when we
become adults?

We want to be grown so bad,

but when we become adults,

we long for that child that's in us to
come out.

You can never get back what you lost,

because you never lost anything.

That little person you saw all those
years is still there

having to face different challenges.

You will win, because of who you are.

# UNFEELING

Sometime people forget that other people have feelings. They act as if other people are not there.

I, as a Black person, had to fight prejudice in my race and outside of my race. No one has control over the way they're born. People act as if they do. For instance, during my lifetime, I have heard people say cruel things about other people.

## Shapes and Sizes

One time, I heard a man say, "She has a nice shape, but I wonder what her face looks like." The woman turned around and in the same breath, the guy said, "Ooh, she ugly."

I was thinking to myself, "Why is he tripping on her shape? What does her face have to do with her body? If she has a nice shape so what? Why are you tripping off it? She has to live with her body everyday."

Another example was what a man said about a woman, "She looks just like a man."

"Haven't you any friends who don't look like men?" I thought. "First, she is a friend, not someone I'm trying to match you up with. Number two, who cares? She's my friend, not yours." Number three, I said to these men, "If she looks like a man, then you better watch out for your job. The only thing she needs is a man's voice."

One time my friend and I were walking down the street. Some

guys asked us about a party. Then one guy in the car said "Those no-toe-wearing tennis shoe girls don't know where a party is."

We kept walking. The other guy got out of the car and he apologized. He said, "I'm sorry. Don't pay any attention to him." He then jumped back into the car and they were gone. Until this day, I never forgot that guy. The biggest thought of all these stories is that these people intruded on other people's lives.

## Hair Weave or Wigs?

Yes, do not let me forget the other story about hair weave or wigs. One day I was on my way to the mall. I was on the bus when a drunken man was "messing" with the bus driver.

The drunk asked, "Is that your real hair?" He was drunk, but that's not the point.

In my mind I kept thinking, "Does it really matter? Did it cost you anything? Why is it so important? Her job is to drive the bus."

# TRIALS

*A message to all my generation:*

Some of our paths will never cross.

Remember that you are a part of me.

Some of you will talk like me.

Some of you will act like me.

But remember we are a family, and no
one dies without leaving a piece of him
here –

even if it is a piece of clothing, or chair,
or couch, or child.

So remember, we live on memories

that we pass on to each generation.

But through our pain and sorrow,

We are still survivors.

That is the mystery of love for each
other.

# KEEP YOU IN MY HEART

We all have grown up,

and we're not children anymore.

We all have gone our separate ways.

It's not that we don't want to be
bothered with each other.

It's just that we have out-grown each
other.

We are no longer children,

so wipe your eyes and dry up those
tears.

We'll always be friends,

we just won't see each other too much.

But we will always keep each other in
thought.

Keep me in your memories, until time
goes on and when you are lonely.  Think
of the good things

we shared with each other as children.

# HANDS

With these hands, I see many things.

I see lines that tell my future,

and lines that go around my hands.

I can make a church with a steeple out
of my cupped hands.

I can open my hands and let the people
in.

I can fold my hands and say a prayer.

I can take my hands

and show warmness with a touch of my
hands.

With these hands, I can show that I care
about a person's feelings.

With these hands, I can perform sign
language to the deaf.  And these hands,
just by the touch

can make me warm.

# LOOKING

Lost souls cry out for help,

but no one hears his or her voices.

So they look up in the sky for answers,

and the only things they see are stars,

and clouds, and silence.

They think to themselves,

"I've been crying for nothing.

I always know the answer – Faith!"

# LOOK INSIDE OF YOURSELF

We can no longer say I'm black and I'm proud," or "Black is beautiful." Black was proud and beautiful, but we have lost our heart.

Our hearts have become like gold: harden with no shine. Our souls have turned to ash. We are lost and we need guidance and understanding for ourselves, and must try to make our lives better by picking up on our inner spirit that tells us what we need to do. First go out and, tell those people next to you, or who lives next door to you, "Let us clean this sidewalk."

Then say, "May I have a drink of water?" That neighbor may give you that glass of water, and your hands touch. You have made the first step and now your hearts have shed a piece of that gold that was hard. Now you see that street shine. It looks different because you decided to change things. That first step is to change your life as you cleaned that street.

# LIFE IS FULL OF PAIN

This is a story about a girl named Ann. Ann was handicapped. She was in a wheelchair. Ann would look out of the window and watch the children playing on swings. Ann would go to bed crying every night. She wanted to walk so badly.

One day someone knocked on the door. Ann's mother let in the visitor. Ann's mother yelled, "Ann, you have company." The little girl sat down. When Ann came into the room in her wheelchair the little girl and Ann started talking.

Ann told the girl, "I wish I could walk as you."

The girl stood up and tripped. Ann noticed that she was blind.

The girl told Ann, "I wish I were you. You have eyes to see. I can only imagine things in my mind."

Ann personally thought that she was feeling sorry for herself. She learned that life is full of pain and that sometimes things are not as bad as they appear in the mind.

# MANY TRAVELS

Books.  So many books.

Where can I be?

I see different stories

and different towns and cities and
animals.
I see different colors of people.

What can I be?  Am I a person or am I
an animal?

Now I know what I am.

I'm a book!

I'm a book with different titles,

many different people, their cultures,
their feelings,

and their pain.

Through my eyes, I can see many
things

and enjoy what I see.

# TIME WASTED

I have no money in my pocket.

The street is my bed.  The trashcan is
my platter.

In the daytime, I sit on the bench, and
watch someone eat a hotdog that looks
as big as a meatloaf.

The water fountain keeps my throat
moist,

and my life has faded in front of me.

The things I took for granted are now
gone.

As I look back, I wasted a lot of time.

Now I'm a face on the street with
nowhere to go.

# THE TREE

Christmas was coming.

I wanted a different Christmas tree.

I didn't want any lights on it.

I wanted to make a Christmas tree out of
dirt, and candy, and candles.

But everyone said,

"You fool.  You can't make a tree out of dirt,
and candy, and candles."

I took a stick, and I drew in the dirt,

and I drew a tree.

Then I wet the dirt and it became mud.

I brought some spice dots of green and red,
purple and orange.

Then I placed candy on the tree.

Then I put candles at each corner of the tree and I put holes in the dirt so they could stand up. At the top of the tree, I placed a candle. I sat on the ground by my Christmas tree.

I started to cry.

I did it;

I had a different Christmas tree.

The thrill lasted me a lifetime because I wanted to be different.

My Christmas tree lasted for two days,

then the snow came and my tree was covered.

I had a vision and it was fulfilled.

That's all that mattered.

I now can keep that tree in my mind and

in my heart forever.

# MESSENGER: TO AN OLD FRIEND

I was remembering the time when we
were kids;

sitting here, thinking about the time we
had.

Now we're old and time has stopped.
The only thing I have is my thoughts of
the past.

I have no sad thoughts, only good
thoughts.

Friends and the treasures we have in
our life

are what keep us strong.

## OPEN YOUR EYES

I see so much pain.

I can't do anything about it.

I want to tell you to have faith.
When you don't have respect you can
get on your knees and pray.

But if you're not true in your heart, it
doesn't mean anything. When was the
last time you said "God, thank you for
giving me the inner strength to open my
eyes each and every day, to see the
sunrise, to smell the air, to see the
trees."?

I know why you never answer the
questions.

You feel that everybody owes you
something – even God.

But you are wrong.  No one said that life was going to be the way you want it to be.

# SADNESS

War never lets you be happy.

War causes homeless children.

War destroys a country.

War causes fear among people.

War causes fear among people.

War causes a lot of "Dear, John" letters.

War sends back half of a man.

War makes a person realize that he has
somebody
back home who cares.

War brings freedom and peace of mind.

# THE BOY AND THE LADYBUG

The boy was playing in the backyard.

A bug was on his shoe.

The little boy looked down.  It was a
ladybug –

red, with black dots.

He picked the bug off  his shoe and

held the bug in the palm of his hand.

He noticed that the bug could talk.

He asked the bug, "Why do people like
killing you when you're not hurting
anyone?"

"I make friends with little boys like you,"
the bug replied.

"But when you become a man,

I'm no longer fun to be with.

I'm a nuisance to you."

# PAIN

Pain comes in so many shapes.

Pain can be a loss of a loved one.

Pain can be a broken leg.

Pain can be a burned hand by a pot.

Pain can be a slap in the face.

Pain can be a loss of a job.

Pain can be a broken heart.

Pain can be healed in many ways.

Without pain, we could not survive.

So when you hear the word pain,

Many things come to your mind.

Next time you hear or have been
touched by pain, remember you will
survive these shapes.

# PEACEFUL

I had so much strength when I was
young.

Now I feel like a little weakling.

Where did my strength go?

Did I get caught in this web?
Was I trying to please everyone?

But my heart was crying out.

No one could hear me, only my mind.

I got up out of my chair and walked on
my porch.

I looked around and saw

how peaceful and quiet it was.

I thought to myself,

It's good to be alive and smell the air

and have peace of mind.  Just in that
quick second –

No worry, just joy.

# SUFFERING HEART

I heard many people talk about my welfare.

While they are arguing, I'm dying very fast.

I have had my first cigarette.

I have had my first joint.

I have killed my first victim.

Now I'm drowning in pity.

Everyone worry about what color I am, but
no one sees my pain.


I called for help.  No one heard my cry.
They're too into themselves
to care about me.

So they wonder why my mind wonders.

I see my father out of work.  He doesn't
want my help.

I see my mother, a woman at forty, looking as if she's sixty with tears in her eyes.

Then I hear on the news that people like us don't want anything.  But if I were a sports person, they'd praise me.

But just because I'm an average person, I'm nothing.

They make me feel like nothing.

They burn out the light that was in me.

Now I have vanished.

The only people who will miss me are the ones I touch during my life.

# STONE HORSE

I'm a stone horse.

People like patting me on my head.

If I could talk, I would let people know
how I feel.

I think people just love to touch me.

They put their fingers in my eye.

They pat me as if I were a dog.

I wish they knew how I felt.

If they could see in my heart,

They would see the pain inside of me.

Just because I'm stone, they think I
have no feelings.

It was just a thought.

We all know that stone can't talk.

# A DREAM

Every time I tried to go to sleep,

I felt death or sickness around the
corner –

Scared to close my eyes;

wondering if time was running out for
me.

Never knowing joy and happiness.

Afraid to smile.

Afraid to laugh.

My inner thoughts took over my mind.

I felt I was going crazy.

Was I mad?

What happened to my thoughts?

I only had bad thoughts. Something was
not right.

I was just having a nightmare.

# A HOMELESS CRY

I stand in front of this building

With my cup in my hand -

out of a job and with an empty pocket,

asking for help, not for me, but for
people like me.

When I was a child, I saw these people -

never thinking that I'd be in this spot.

It's funny how we walk pass these
people as children.
Then we become them.

So don't walk away because one day,

You may be walked away from too.

# Autobiography
By Annette Eloise Riley Joseph

*I was born in St. Louis, Missouri (MO) as Annette Eloise Joseph.*

*I am a mother of four and I came from a paternal family that consisted of two brothers and one sister. One brother is deceased.*

*My mother, Doris Vails Riley, felt that education was very important to her children. However, I personally felt education was not very important to me. But it's interesting of all of my mother's children, I went to school the most.*

*She graduated from Curtis School in 1966. The school at that time was located at 2824 Madison. (See inside front of book.)*

*Later I also graduated from Central High School, 3916 North Garrison in January 1971. Then I attended Forest Park College at 5600 Oakland (1974-1982) and finally Harris Stowe College.*

*Continuing my studies I enrolled in the Academy of Beauty and graduated in 1995. I later attended and graduated from a three-year program at Parkside Tower with a CNA (Certified Nurse Associate) degree.*

*Professionally I have tutored children, been a substitute teacher, and worked as a cafeteria aide. Some work was done with the St. Louis Association for Retarded Citizens in 1998, and the Gateway State School for Handicapped Children in 1982.*

*I graduated from St. Louis College of Health Careers as a medical assistant in 2002.*

*As a volunteer, I worked at the South Pointe Hospital (1997) and as a volunteer at the St. Louis Tutor Workshop.*

*In June, 2004, as a writer, I entered a poetry-writing contest and eventually completed my first poetry collections book in 2005.*

# A Tear
## From The Corner
### of Her Eye

# A MESSAGE TO MY CHILD

An emotional-feeling arose.

Time was coming fast and the baby was
coming into our world.

The nurse brought the baby to his
mother.

The mother whispered in his ear and
said,

"This is a cruel world.

I love you.

The tears that I shed for you now,

I will never shed them again.

I have done my crying for you.

Each tear is a pain and I can't cry
anymore.

My heart is empty and you can now face
the world."